D0493157

Sweet Cherry Publishing Limited
Unit 36, Vulcan House,
Vulcan Road,
Leicester, LE5 3EF
United Kingdom

Published in 2019

2 4 6 8 10 9 7 5 3 1

ISBN: 978-1-78226-589-4

© &™ 2019. Aardman Animations Ltd. & Studiocanal SAS.
'Shaun the Sheep Movie Farmageddon' (word mark),
'Shaun the Sheep' (word mark) and the character 'Shaun
the Sheep' are trademarks used under licence from
Aardman Animations Limited, all rights reserved.

Written by Gemma Barder

Printed and manufactured in Turkey
Print code T.IO006

This annual belongs to

A Shaun the Sheep MOVIE

FARMAGEDDON™

ANNUAL 2020

Sweet Cherry

CONTENTS

MEET
SHAUN!

Mossy Bottom Farm's Cheekiest Flock Member

NAME: Shaun the Sheep
OCCUPATION: Having as much fun as possible – without the Farmer knowing
BEST FRIEND: Lu-La

FARMAGEDDON FACT! Although Shaun can be a bit mischievous, he's a very caring sheep who always tries to help friends in need.

Shaun likes doing three things: getting up to mischief with the Flock, eating and teasing Bitzer. Life on the farm is pretty chilled, until Shaun meets Lu-La. Now Shaun's mysterious new friend is about to turn his life upside down.
Can Shaun help this adorable alien before it's too late? It's time for his biggest challenge yet!

FARMAGEDDON FACT! Shaun is impressed with Lu-La's eating habits. He didn't think anyone could devour food as quickly as him!

FARMAGEDDON FACT! Shaun can ride a BMX bike - or at least he would if Bitzer didn't stop him all the time!

A STRANGE NEW FRIEND

Shaun loved living on Mossy Bottom Farm ... well, he did *most* of the time. Today, Shaun was not happy. He and the Flock had come up with lots of new ways to have fun, but Bitzer had put a stop to every single one of them. The dog was so angry that he had sent the whole Flock back to the barn with nothing but sheep nuts for dinner.

IT WAS SO UNFAIR! WHY DIDN'T HE LIKE HAVING FUN?

Shaun couldn't sleep. His tummy was rumbling so much it hurt. The rumbling got **LOUDER** and **LOUDER**. Wait ... it wasn't just Shaun's tummy! He went to the window. How strange – there was a line of black vans heading into Mossingham. As Shaun turned away, he saw something move in the field. He looked again. Nothing. Shaun shrugged and went back to bed.

The next morning, most of the Flock ran out to breakfast, but Shaun was tired. He trudged along after them. Oh, great – they had eaten everything. Shaun wandered grumpily away from the empty trough, then stopped. At his feet was a half-eaten pizza. He looked up.

THERE WAS ANOTHER! AND ANOTHER!

Shaun followed the trail back into the barn.

Inside, Shaun could hear a shuffling sound. He edged towards it. There was a figure hidden in the shadows. She moved into a strip of light. She had big purple eyes, floppy pink ears and a long, blue body. Shaun blinked. Pink floppy ears? *Purple* eyes?!

SHAUN HAD NEVER SEEN ANYONE STRANGER.

'ARGH!!!' Shaun and the creature screamed at each other.

Not knowing what else to do, Shaun nervously offered the creature the slice of pizza he was holding. She gobbled it up. This creature wasn't scary! Shaun giggled. She giggled back. It was a perfect impression of Shaun.

Shaun introduced her to his friends. The Flock liked the funny blue creature. It was very funny when she hid in Shirley's wool, and they loved her impressions.

Bitzer was having a normal day. An everyday sort of day. He went to fetch the Farmer's mail. On his way back, he passed the Flock who suddenly became very well-behaved. In Bitzer's experience, there was nothing more suspicious than well-behaved sheep. He went closer to them.

Shaun smiled and waved at Bitzer. He couldn't help but notice the front page of the newspaper he was holding.

MOSSINGHAM LOCAL GAZETT
UFO!

THAT WAS IT! THE CREATURE MUST BE AN ALIEN!

11

PICK A PIZZA PATH

Shaun has ordered a stack of delicious pizzas to Mossy Bottom Farm. Find a clear path to help the delivery boy get to the barn before the pizzas go cold. Avoid any dead ends or paths that lead to obstacles!

START

END

YOUR SLICE OR MINE?

PIZZA OFFERS!

FARMAGEDDON FACT!

In America, they eat **300 ACRES** of pizza a DAY! This would cover the fields at Mossy Bottom Farm three times over!

Finally, the Flock has something good to eat. But, oh no! The slices got jumbled up on the back of the delivery bike.

Can you match each slice to its identical pair? Once you've finished there should be one left over. (You can have this one, you've earned it!)

£££££!

PIZZA OFFER

Open Every Day
Monday - Friday 12:00 PM - 11:
Saturday 1:00 PM - 11:30
Sunday 3:00 PM - 11:00

A B C D

E F G

H I

ANSWERS:

I get to eat

FRISBEE FUN

The Flock have some energy to burn off after all of that pizza. Time for a quick game of frisbee!

Find all 12 differences between the two pictures and circle them before Bitzer makes the Flock stop playing.

CROP CIRCLES

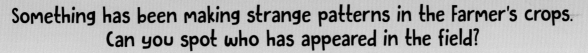

Something has been making strange patterns in the farmer's crops.
Can you spot who has appeared in the field?

MEET
LU-LA!

Mossy Bottom Farm's Adorable Alien Visitor

NAME: Lu-La
OCCUPATION: Mossy Bottom Farm's cutest alien visitor
BEST FRIEND: Shaun

FARMAGEDDON FACT! When Lu-La uses her powers, her ears stand up and sparkle.

Lu-La is stranded on Earth, millions of miles away from her home planet. Although she's desperate to get home, this playful little alien is also very curious about our planet. She's already learned what happens when she eats too many sweets - an ear-blasting burp!

Lu-La can also perform out-of-this-world tricks like perfect impressions, and making objects fly around in the air. With Shaun to help her, Lu-La must find her way home before she's discovered, but she's going to have as much fun as possible along the way!

FARMAGEDDON FACT! Lu-La calls her mum and dad Ub-Oo and Me-Ma.

FARMAGEDDON FACT! Lu-La didn't mean to crash-land on Earth. Despite all her powers, she's still a young alien who arrived in Mossingham by mistake!

THE SOLAR SYSTEM

A solar system is a group of planets, comets, moons and asteroids that orbit a star. Earth's solar system orbits around the Sun - which is a big star.

Sun

Our Solar System is made up of eight planets:

Mercury

Venus

Earth

DRAW LU-LA'S HOME PLANET

Lu-La's home planet is a mystery to everyone in Mossingham, including Shaun and the Flock. Use the space above to imagine what it could look like. What colour is the sky? What shape are the trees? What type of homes do they live in?

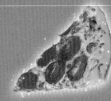

Lu-La tries to show Shaun and the Flock where her home planet is by using her amazing powers to make a model of her solar system.

Mars

Saturn

Uranus

Neptune

Jupiter

LU-LA CREATES!

YOU WILL NEED:
Paper and colouring pencils (optional)
Thread   Scissors
Card   Sticky tape

What would you do if you crash-landed on an alien planet and needed to show your new friends where you came from?

(1) Cut out these images of the planets in our Solar System. If you don't want to cut out this page from your book, you can trace the planets and colour them in instead!

(2) Tape the end of a length of string to your planet, and the other end to a strip of cardboard.

(3) Repeat step 2 for each planet, making sure you put your planets in the correct order.

(4) Ask a grown up to help hang your Solar System from the ceiling, or underneath a shelf.

TAKEAWAY JIGSAW

Lu-La's spaceship crash-landed near the takeaway place,
and she wants to show Shaun where to find it.
Help her to put the takeaway logo back together.

£££££!
PIZZA OFFERS!

WHOSE ORDER?

Match the pizza to the character who ordered it. We've left one pizza blank for you to add your own dream toppings ...

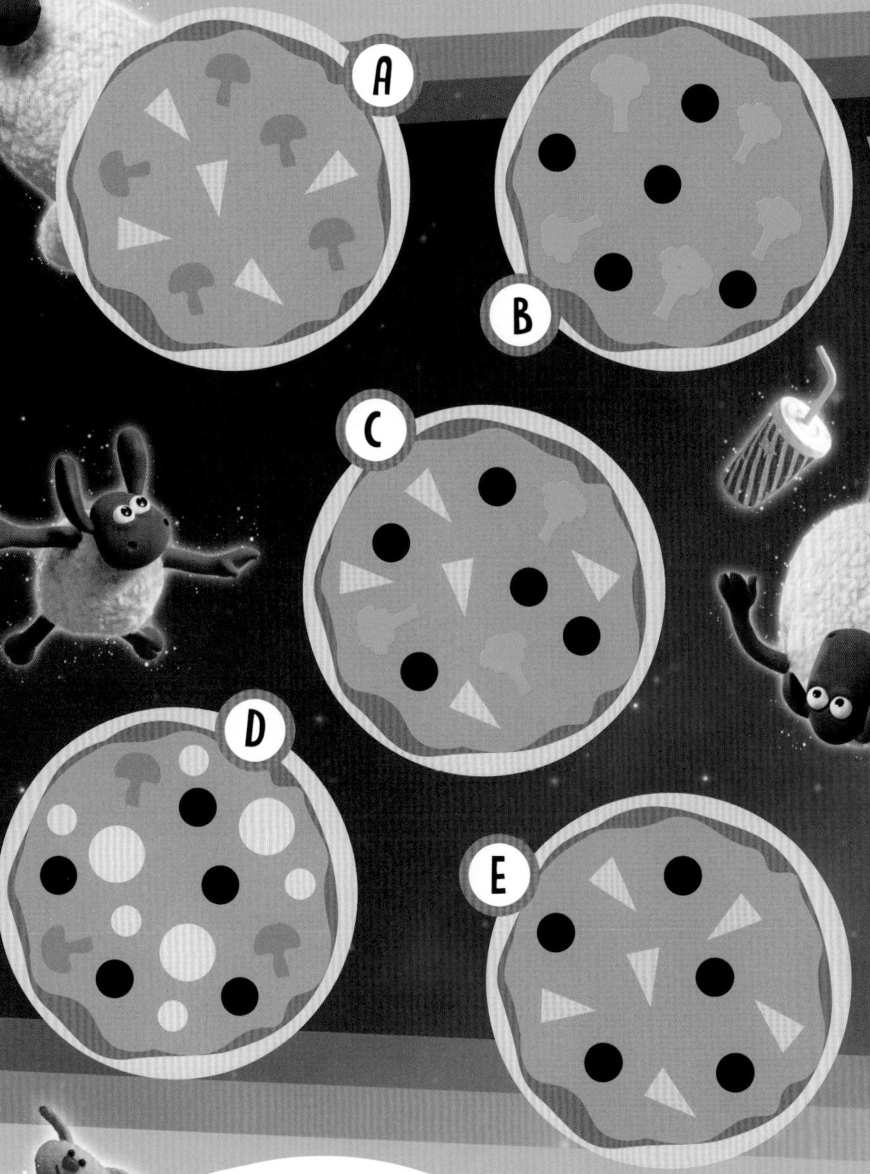

A

B

C

D

E

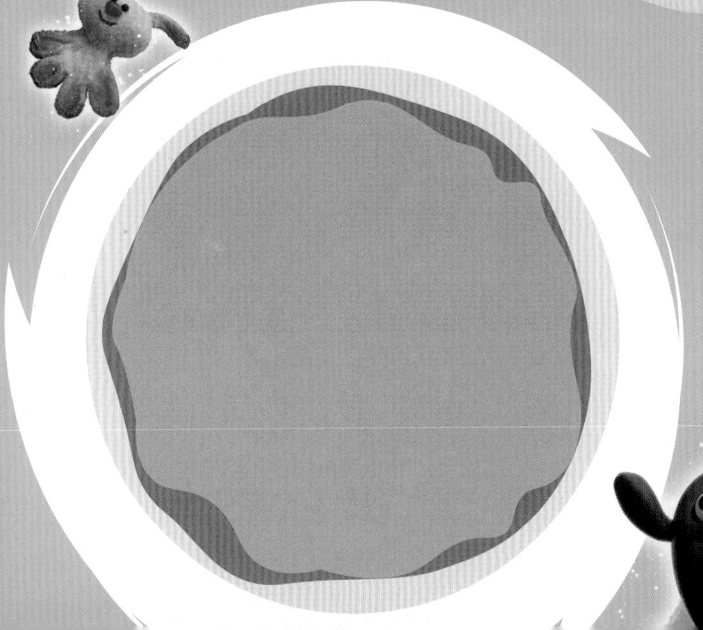

SHAUN
Mushroom, cheese and olives! 

TIMMY
Pineapple and mushroom

TIMMY'S MUM
Broccoli and olives

NUTS
Pineapple and olives

SHIRLEY
Pineapple, olives and broccoli.

IT'S A SIGN!

Bitzer has had enough of the Flock's messing about.
It's time he put a stop to them throwing frisbees,
playing on the combine harvester, jumping over each
other on bikes, hot air ballooning ... and having fun.
Help Bitzer to put his signs back together.

ANSWERS:

A

B

C

D

E

F

G

H

I

J

BAN IT!

Bitzer has left a blank sign behind. What would you like to ban if you could? Broccoli? Homework? Brushing your teeth? Use Bitzer's spare sign to create your own design!

Disclaimer: We can't promise that making this sign will mean you'll never have to brush your teeth again. Sorry about that!

WHICH FARMAGEDDON CHARACTER ARE YOU?

Answer the questions, add up your answers, then get ready for your woolly-coat fitting. Time to find your place in the Flock.

1. WHAT'S THE FIRST THING YOU DO IN THE MORNING?

○ **A.** Eat breakfast and plan something fun for the day.

✓ **C.** A big yawn and wonder what's for breakfast.

○ **B.** Get up, get dressed, and sort out your school bag.

○ **D.** Give your parents a big cuddle.

2. WHAT'S THE BEST PART OF THE DAY?

✓ **A.** Mealtimes, and any time you can have fun!

○ **C.** Being outside for PE or at playtime.

○ **B.** Giving in your homework - you can't wait to see how you've done.

○ **D.** Any time you are with friends or family.

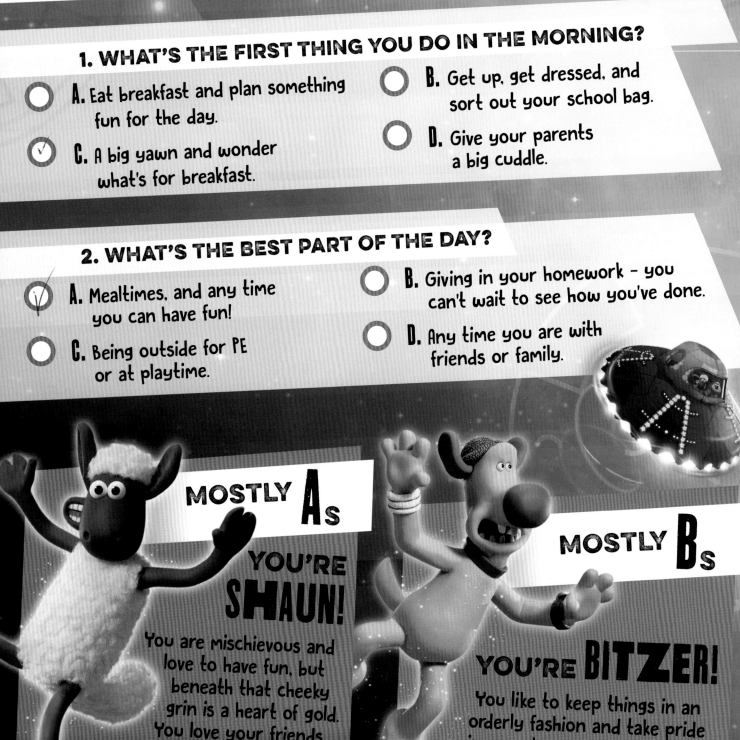

MOSTLY **A**s

YOU'RE SHAUN!

You are mischievous and love to have fun, but beneath that cheeky grin is a heart of gold. You love your friends and would do anything to help them out.

MOSTLY **B**s

YOU'RE BITZER!

You like to keep things in an orderly fashion and take pride in your homework, but you're also super caring and look out for your friends.

3. WHAT DO YOU DO WHEN YOU MEET SOMEONE NEW?

A. Give them a big hug and ask them to play with you.

C. Shake their hand, firmly. ✓

B. Ask them a few questions to get to know them.

D. Smile shyly and hope they like you.

4. WHAT DO YOU LIKE BEST ABOUT SCHOOL?

A. Coming home!

C. PE and lunchtime.

B. Learning something new. ✓

D. Spending time with your friends.

5. WHICH THREE WORDS DESCRIBE YOU BEST?

A. Fun, cheeky, loyal.

C. Imaginative, leader, outdoorsy. ✓

B. Hardworking, neat, kind.

D. Sweet, friendly, happy.

6. WHAT SORT OF FRIEND ARE YOU?

A. You've got lots of best friends. People just seem to like you! ✓

C. You don't have one best friend, you get along with everyone the same.

B. You've had the same best friend for a long time.

D. Family comes first, then friends.

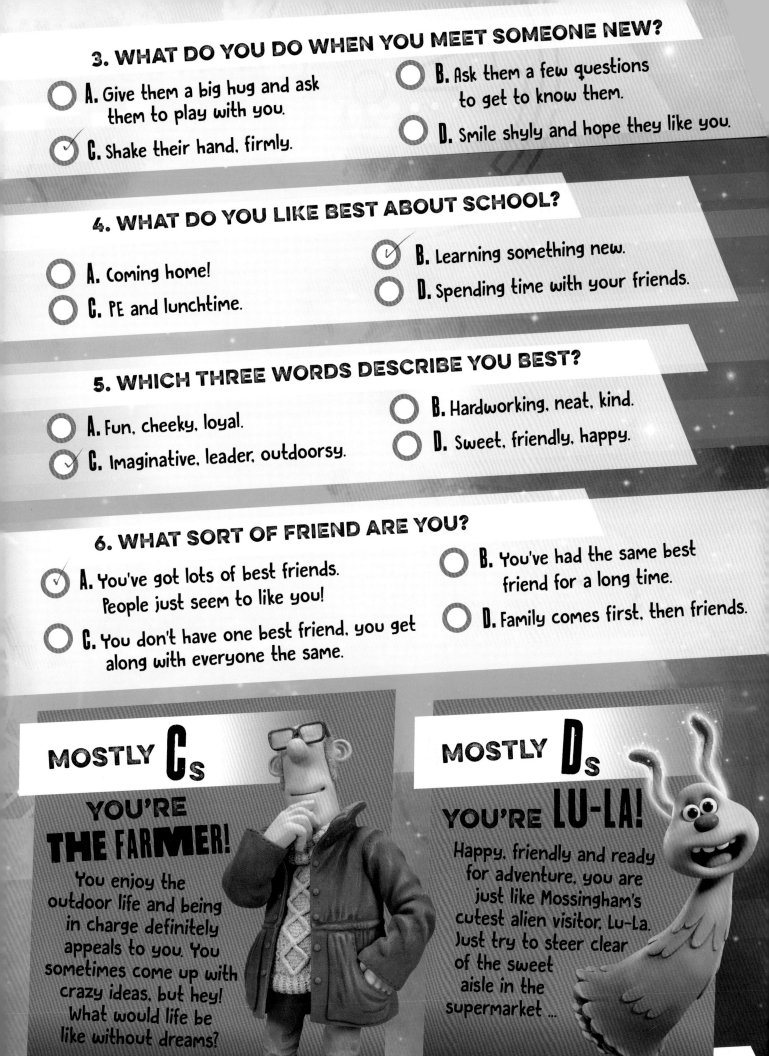

MOSTLY Cs

YOU'RE THE FARMER!

You enjoy the outdoor life and being in charge definitely appeals to you. You sometimes come up with crazy ideas, but hey! What would life be like without dreams?

MOSTLY Ds

YOU'RE LU-LA!

Happy, friendly and ready for adventure, you are just like Mossingham's cutest alien visitor, Lu-La. Just try to steer clear of the sweet aisle in the supermarket ...

25

MEET
BITZER!

Mossy Bottom Farm's Biggest Worrier

NAME: Bitzer
OCCUPATION: Mossy Bottom Farm's sheepdog
BEST FRIEND: The Farmer (and Shaun and the Flock when they are behaving themselves!)

FARMAGEDDON FACT! Bitzer and Shaun have known each other since they were young and grew up together on the farm.

It's Bitzer's job to keep the Flock in check, just like the good sheepdog that he is. This can mean anything from stopping a runaway combine harvester to banning the Flock from making sheep pyramids. Bitzer also has to help the Farmer with all his plans! Bitzer has to keep the Flock under control, build a theme-park and be in the Farmer's play. He also has to wear very silly-looking astronaut suit, all while keeping an eye on what Shaun is getting up to. It's not easy being Bitzer!

FARMAGEDDON FACT! Bitzer was given his blue woolly hat by the Farmer when he was a puppy.

FARMAGEDDON FACT! Although he can be a bit strict sometimes, Bitzer cares about the Flock and would never tell the Farmer about the mischief they get up to.

MEET THE NEIGHBOURS

When Lu-La crash-lands on Earth, Shaun and the Flock are taken by surprise. Could you get to meet an alien visitor one day, too?

WHERE COULD ALIENS EXIST?

For life like ours to survive, a planet needs to have water, warmth and light. Lu-La's planet has all of these things, which is why she feels at home on Earth. We don't know what alien life might look like - they could be anything, from tiny cells, to giant walking plants!

DRAW YOUR ALIEN!

What do YOU think aliens look like? Draw your idea in the space below.

STRANGE SIGHTINGS

PEARL PRESENCE

One of the earliest records of an alien encounter was in 1088 in the Chinese city of Yangzhou. The story tells of a strange vessel opening its doors to reveal a pearl-shaped object that cast a bright light all around it. Then the light dashed off again at high speed!

ANGELIC ALIEN

In 1917, in the Portuguese town of Fátima, three children said they saw a figure which floated like an angel. The figure appeared briefly once more to a gathering of townspeople, who believed it was a religious encounter. However, some people believe the figure could have been an alien.

NOW YOU SEE THEM, NOW YOU DON'T!

In 2011, a security guard from South Dakota spotted creatures on the side of the road as he drove home from work. They looked like people, but with very long arms and legs - oh, and you could see straight through them! The creatures disappeared when another car came along the road.

TALK TO ALIENS!

Lu-La and Shaun quickly realise that they can't understand each other. Shaun has an important message for the adorable alien - can you work out what he's trying to say?

A HUMONGOUS BURP

Lu-La was disappointed. Her new friends were great, but they didn't understand anything she said. She grabbed a stick and drew a picture of her home planet in the dust. Maybe this would work? She looked at Shaun.

HE STARED BACK IN CONFUSION.

Lu-La had an idea. Wiggling her long ears, she sent random things flying up into the air and floating round in the shape of her solar system. Next, she made a spaceship out of a toilet seat, a hubcap, and a jam jar lid. She drew a symbol in the dirt and sent the model spaceship crashing into it.

Lu-La was telling Shaun where her spaceship was! Why did that symbol look familiar? Of course!

THE FOREST TAKEAWAY!

He grabbed a menu. At the top was the same symbol Lu-La had drawn. Shaun and Lu-La looked at each other.

THIS WAS WHERE THEY NEEDED TO GO.

Before long, Shaun and Lu-La were heading into Mossingham at high speed - in a big yellow bin. As it rolled to a stop, Shaun peeked out. There were a lot of people about. If anyone spotted Lu-La, they would want to catch and study her and then she would never get back to her ship. Shaun was going to have to keep a close eye on the alien ... Where was she?!

Lu-La's eyes widened as she walked into the supermarket. She had never seen anything like it! Shaun dashed over. He beckoned to Lu-La, but she was already munching happily on a toilet roll.

SHAUN ROLLED HIS EYES AND FOLLOWED LU-LA IN.

The sweets aisle was a beautiful mix of neon colours. It looked like the fruit from Lu-La's home planet – delicious! She grabbed as many sweets as possible and stuffed them into her mouth. After munching for a few moments, Lu-La started to feel funny ...

Lu-La's ears waggled. Shaun braced himself; this wasn't going to end well. Lu-La took off in a hurricane of energy, whizzing around the shop and sending food flying. When she stopped, Lu-La let out an **INTERGALACTIC BURP,** which sent the supermarket shelves toppling down like dominoes. Shaun and Lu-La made a swift exit before anyone could work out what had happened.

Lu-La and Shaun ran past the Forest Takeaway, and into the forest. They stopped at an open clearing. Lu-La was excited, but Shaun couldn't see why. There was nothing there! Lu-La rushed into the clearing. Then, she disappeared. Moments later, the air started to shimmer. Suddenly, a gleaming spaceship appeared.

IT HAD BEEN INVISIBLE!

Shaun followed his friend on board. He couldn't believe he was actually inside an **ALIEN SPACESHIP!**

SUPERMARKET MUDDLE

Lu-La and Shaun are in Mossingham Supermarket. Draw a path to help them to find their way out. Make sure you avoid the sweets along the way, though, or Lu-La will never get out of there!

EXIT

LU-LA'S MESSAGE

Lu-La needs to tell Shaun something, urgently! Can you work out what she is saying?

Circle every letter that isn't an L or a U in the words below.

LSULLWLELELTULS
LULALURLEULL
LUALLMLULUALUZULLILLUNLUG!
LCUALLUUNL
LIU
LUHLLULUALLUUVUULLE
SLLUOLLUMULULE
LUMLLUUOULLURLLUELLU?
LULTLLHUULLALULNLULKLLUSLL!

SWEETS ARE AMAZING! CAN I
HAVE SOME MORE? THANKS!

CREATE YOUR OWN CODE!

Try making up your own coded message. You could use numbers for letters, write words backwards, or even come up with your own alphabet. Just make sure the person you are sending your message to knows how to crack your code!

FARMAGEDDON
SUDOKU

Can you fit each of the characters below into these grids? They can only appear once in every column, and once in every row.

Use the characters initials to help you fill in the grids.

S

B

L

AR

THROUGH THE FOREST

Lu-La has guided Shaun to the forest where her spaceship crash-landed! All they need to do now, is find it. Follow the instructions and make a mark when you think you have found the spot!

Right 3 spaces
Down 2 spaces
Left 2 spaces
Down 1 space
Right 4 spaces
Down 2 spaces
Left 1 space
Up 1 space

MEET AGENT RED!

She's on a mission and won't let anything stand in her way.

NAME: Agent Red
OCCUPATION: Ministry of Alien Detection Agent
BEST FRIEND: She claims to work alone, but she couldn't do without her robot sidekick, MUGG-IN5

FARMAGEDDON FACT! Her favourite shade of lipstick is called Renegade Red.

As soon as Agent Red hears about the strange sightings over Mossingham, she dashes over to investigate. Agent Red is convinced that aliens really do exist no matter what anyone else says. Assisted by the Hazmats, and with a highly intelligent (though clumsy) robot, MUGG-IN5, by her side, she's determined to find proof.

FARMAGEDDON FACT! Agent Red has travelled the world in search of UFOs and alien encounters.

FARMAGEDDON FACT! Agent Red's history with aliens started a long time before she worked for the Ministry.

ON THE HUNT
FOR DIFFERENCES!

Agent Red and Farmer John are on the trail of Lu-La's spaceship.

Take a look at these two pictures and see if you can spot the **12 DIFFERENCES** between them.

FIND LU-LA AND SHAUN!

Shaun and Lu-La need to keep out of sight if they want to avoid Agent Red. Can you find them, plus all the other items on the list?

Shaun

Lu-La

Pizza box

Frisbee

Sweets

Football

BMX bike

Pizza slice

UFOS

Lu-La's spaceship can travel millions of miles across space, but have any other alien spaceships travelled to Earth?

ALIEN VISITOR CASE ONE: V STRANGE!

TOP SECRET
1

In 2001, motorists outside New Jersey stopped to stare at a set of yellow and orange lights that had formed a giant 'V' in the sky. There were lots of witnesses, including a police officer. Most of them believe the lights were not from this planet.

ALIEN VISITOR CASE TWO: ELECTRIC ATMOSPHERE

TOP SECRET
2

In 1957, residents of a small town in Texas reported seeing strange lights, followed by electricity and car failures. The police put it down to an electrical storm, even though there weren't any thunderstorms in the area that night. Could it have been the work of mischievous aliens?

DESIGN YOUR OWN UFO

Imagine you were about to go on a mission to discover strange new planets. What would your spaceship look like? What would you take with you? What cool gadgets would you need? Use the space below to create your own UFO!

SPOT THE UFOS!

Looks like we have more alien visitors! Can you find all 12 of the UFOs hiding on these two pages? Circle them as you find them.

FARMAGEDDON FACT!

In science fiction stories, UFOs often travel at the speed of light. This is **186,282 MILES PER SECOND** (299,792 km per second). No human has travelled at this speed yet, but scientists are trying to work out how it could be done.

FIND THE FOB!

To get back home, Lu-La needs the fob key that starts her spaceship. Can you help Shaun and Lu-La find the right one?

42

DRAW LU-LA AND BITZER!

Use the grid to copy these pictures of Lu-La and Bitzer square by square.
Once you've finished, you can colour them in.

PANIC UNDERGROUND!

Agent Red had always dreamed of discovering alien life. Finally, she was coming close. She'd found an actual spaceship in Mossingham! All she had to do now was get into it.

Meanwhile, Shaun was having the best day of his life. He was inside a *real* spaceship! With a *real* alien! But the alien was panicking. Lu-La pointed to an empty slot. Oh no! Her ship wouldn't go anywhere without its special fob.

Shaun looked round, searching for the fob. He spotted a framed picture of Lu-La with two bigger aliens. Lu-La was between them, clutching an alien teddy. Lu-La was a child! **WHY WAS SHE HERE ALL ALONE?** Lu-La turned to Shaun. She used her alien powers to show him how she had accidentally sent the spaceship across the galaxy.

Shaun sighed. Lu-La was desperate to get home, but without the fob he didn't know what to do. Before he had a chance to think, the spaceship began to shake. They rushed to the window. They certainly weren't in the forest anymore!

The spaceship had been moved to an underground base. It was crawling with people wearing yellow hazmat suits. Lu-La's eyes grew wide. Agent Red was holding her fob. She looked desperately at Shaun.

Shaun told Lu-La to stay put. He tip-toed out of the spaceship and followed Agent Red to her office. She whistled a secret tune to unlock the door. If only he could whistle like that ...

Suddenly, Shaun heard the same whistle again. He turned around - Lu-La had followed him! They slipped inside the office.

Lu-La used her ears to levitate the fob. Shaun shook his head at her. They were being too obvious. Agent Red would notice *that*! Lu-La's concentration broke and the fob fell to the ground.

Back on the spaceship, there was another problem: an unexpected passenger. Bitzer had spotted Shaun and Lu-La in Mossingham. He had followed them onto the spaceship and got trapped. Luckily, the fob had landed on a button that let him out.

Still wearing the silly alien costume the Farmer had given him, Bitzer left the spaceship.

EVERYONE THOUGHT HE WAS A REAL ALIEN!

The commotion drew Agent Red to the window. Perfect! While she shouted instructions through the glass, Shaun and Lu-La grabbed the fob and ran back into the spaceship.

Shaun didn't have time to explain anything to Bitzer.

THEY HAD TO GET OUT OF THE BASE.

Shaun pressed random buttons on the control pad. One of them was bound to do *something*. Bitzer watched in shock as they hurtled into space.

The autopilot sign pinged on. The passengers looked at each other. The spaceship was taking them home ... but it wasn't heading to Mossy Bottom Farm.

IT WAS HEADING TO LU-LA'S PLANET!

MEET THE FLOCK!

A Close-Knit Bunch of Friends!

NAME: The Flock
OCCUPATIONS: Growing wool and eating grass
BEST FRIENDS: Each other!

FARMAGEDDON FACT! Sheep can recognise different bleats. So, a mother sheep can call to her lamb, and the lamb will know who it is.

The Flock are one big happy family. They live on Mossy Bottom Farm and love to make mischief. Timmy wants to be just like Shaun. Timmy's Mum makes sure Timmy doesn't get into too much trouble and enjoys a spot of knitting. Shirley is happy to go along with Shaun's plans, as long as she gets something to eat at the end of it all.

Hazel's nerves often get the better of her, but she's braver than she thinks, and Nuts is ... well ... Nuts. The Flock are a bit scared of Lu-La to begin with, but they soon accept her with open hooves.

FARMAGEDDON FACT! Without the Flock, Bitzer would be out of a job. It is up to him to keep them all in line.

FARMAGEDDON FACT! Sheep produce one fleece a year which is turned into wool. Each fleece produces between 900 grams - 13 kilograms of wool.

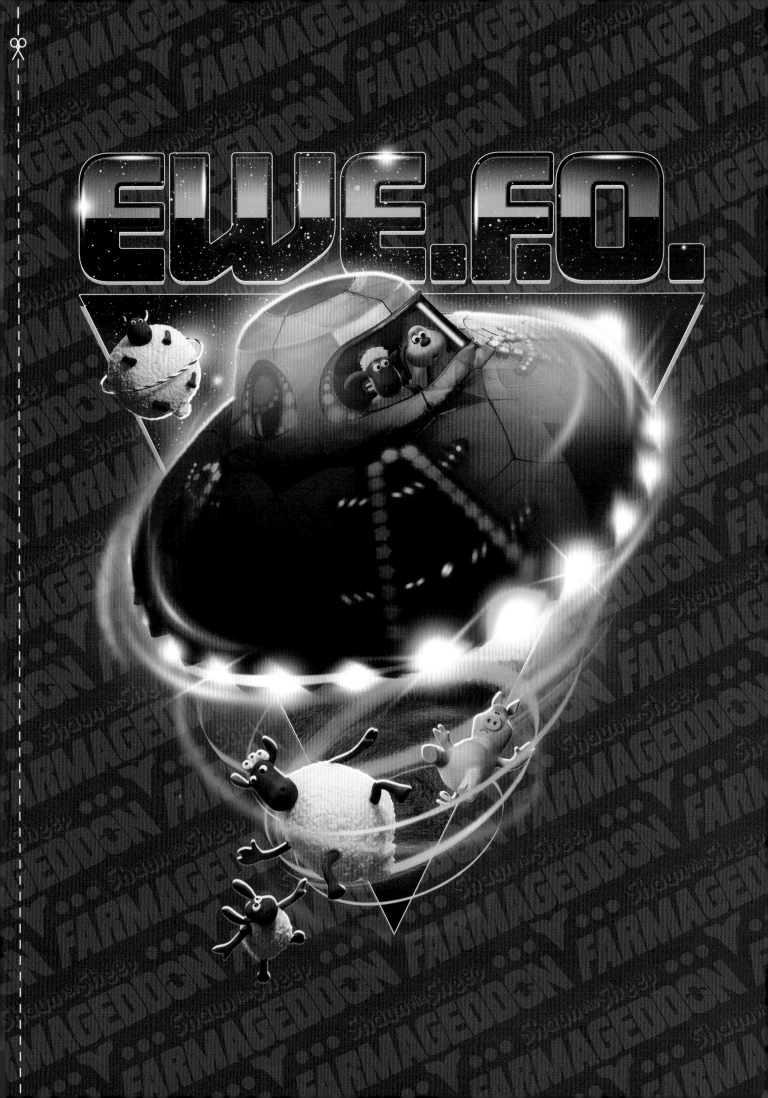

WHAT'S YOUR DREAM LIFE ON MOSSY BOTTOM FARM?

The inhabitants of Mossy Bottom Farm all have their own dreams – some big, some small. Answer the questions to work out yours!

1. YOU'VE SPOTTED SOME STRANGE LIGHTS IN THE NIGHT SKY. WHAT DO YOU DO?

☆ Go and investigate!

▢ Ask your family if they saw them, too.

📖 Check the weather report for storms. It was probably lightening.

2. YOUR BEST FRIEND THINKS THEY'VE SPOTTED A UFO. DO YOU BELIEVE THEM?

📖 You think UFOs could exist. You've read about them in books.

☆ Of course! You write down a detailed description of what they saw.

▢ You ask them about it, but don't really believe them.

3. IF YOU MET AN ALIEN, WHAT WOULD YOU DO?

▢ Immediately call your friends to come and take a look.

☆ Try to communicate with them in any way you can.

📖 Call your parents, then research online what the creature is, because you're not sure aliens are real.

4. IF YOU COULD GO ANYWHERE ON HOLIDAY, WHERE WOULD YOU GO?

☆ The International Space Station

📖 The beach

▢ Disney World

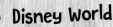

5. IT'S THE WEEKEND AND YOUR FRIENDS WANT TO SPEND TIME WITH YOU. WHAT DO YOU WANT TO DO?

- Ride your bike to the park
- Go to the cinema
- Look for snails in the garden and build them a nice new home

6. IF YOU WERE FAMOUS, IT WOULD BE FOR...

- Writing books
- Creating a video game or app
- Making a scientific discovery

MOSTLY TICKETS

LIKE SHAUN,

you love having as much fun as possible. Your dream adventure would be to open your own theme park, just like Farmageddon! You would love to design the rides and you would invite all of your friends to join you!

MOSTLY STARS

JUST LIKE LU-LA,

you are a bit of an adventurer. You'd love to be an astronaut one day and explore other planets. Who knows? One day you might meet your own alien friend!

MOSTLY BOOKS

You like to escape into books for your adventures. **JUST LIKE BITZER,** your dream is to be surrounded by a cosy home, with the people you love. You don't mind if you miss out on climbing a mountain, or jetting into space.

49

PRESS THE BUTTON

Lu-La needs to press the right button on the control panel to start her spaceship. Put the pieces of this puzzle back together to help her.

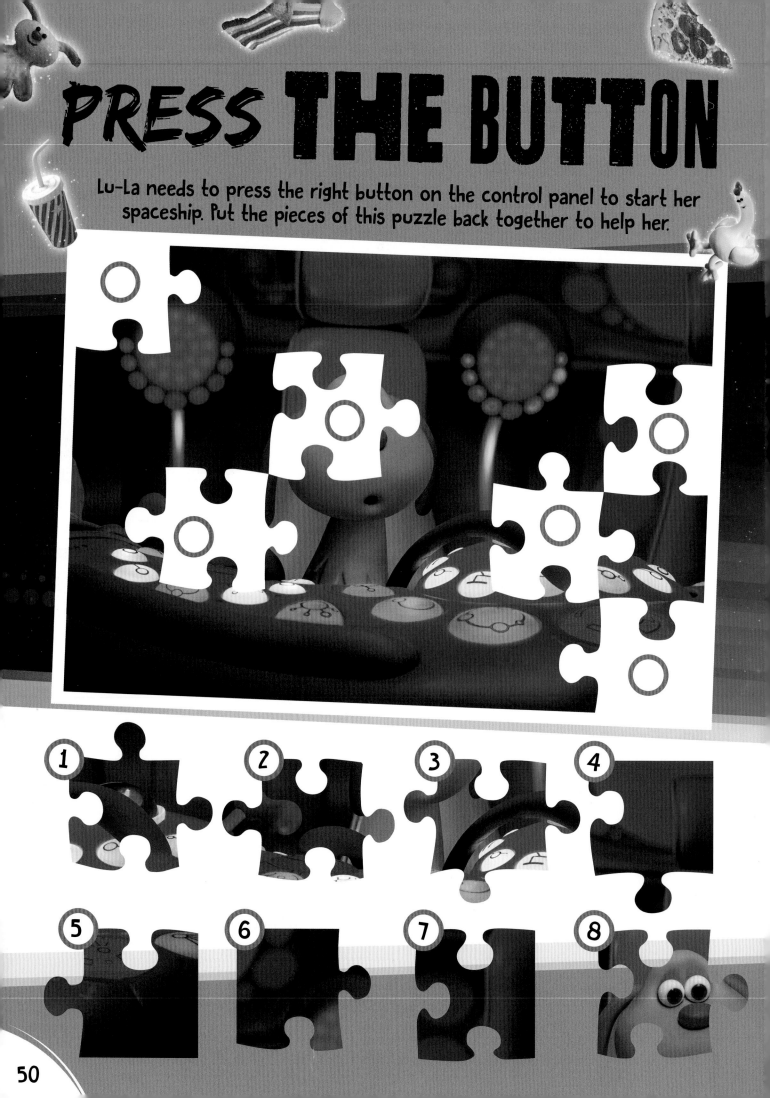

ERROR!

Something has gone wrong! The spaceship won't start up and there is a strange message on the control deck. Can you work out what it says? Use the space below to write down each letter of the message.

A B C D E F G H I J K L M N

O P Q R S T U V W X Y Z

_ _ _ _ _ _ ! _ _ _ _ _ _ _ _ _ _

_ _ _ _ _ _ _ _ _ _ _ .

TOP SECRET!

MUGG-IN5 has dropped Agent Red's top-secret files. Can you put them into the correct piles? There should be five files in each pile.

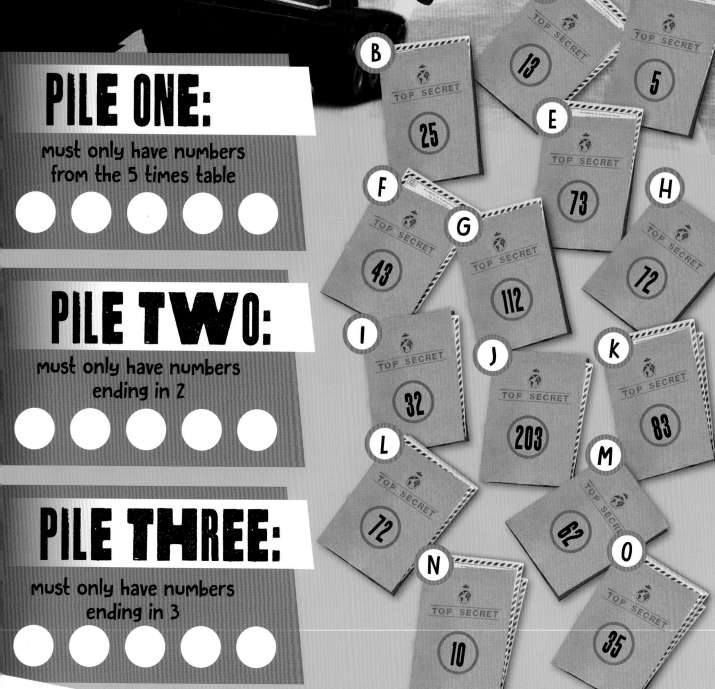

PILE ONE:
must only have numbers from the 5 times table

◯ ◯ ◯ ◯ ◯

PILE TWO:
must only have numbers ending in 2

◯ ◯ ◯ ◯ ◯

PILE THREE:
must only have numbers ending in 3

◯ ◯ ◯ ◯ ◯

A 15
B 25
C 13
D 5
E 73
F 43
G 112
H 72
I 32
J 203
K 83
L 72
M 62
N 10
O 35

TICKETS, PLEASE!

The Farmer is about to start selling tickets to the Farmageddon theme park. There is one space left for a ride and you get to design it!

Will it be indoors or outdoors?

FARMAGEDDON

How will you make it alien and space-themed?

Use the space below to create your very own ride!

It could be a roller coaster, a 3D ride or even a water flume!

Draw a poster to advertise your ride, too!

READ ALL ABOUT IT!

All the strange happenings in Mossingham have made the front page of the Farmer's newspaper. Write an exciting report and draw a picture, too!

MOSSINGHAM LOCAL GAZETTE

EXCLUSIVE SPECIAL REPORT INSIDE!

DRAW SHAUN!

Use the grid to copy this picture of Shaun square by square. Once you've finished, you can colour him in.

FARMAGEDDON FACT!

Shaun once had all the wool shorn off him, so he had to wear a little knitted jumper instead!

55

MEET THE FARMER!

NAME: The Farmer
OCCUPATION: Um ... a farmer!
BEST FRIEND: Bitzer

FARMAGEDDON FACT! A long time ago, the Farmer used to be quite a good dancer!

The Farmer loves his farm. He spends most of his time working on the land, trying to shear his sheep, and looking after his animals. The Farmer has known Bitzer since he was a puppy. He's a little bit clumsy and sometimes loses his temper when the Flock destroy parts of the farm. When the Farmer hears that everyone is going crazy for aliens, he decides to build the Farmageddon theme park on his land. The Farmer leaves it up to Bitzer and the Flock to build the theme park while he writes a play about Mossingham's alien encounter.

FARMAGEDDON FACT! He has a twin brother who once fooled the Flock into thinking he was the Farmer!

FARMAGEDDON FACT! The Farmer used to be a prize golfer. Bitzer was his caddy (the person who helps carry and choose what clubs the golfer is going to use).

SELFIE SPOT

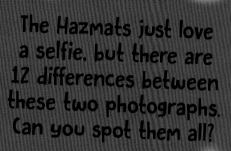

The Hazmats just love a selfie, but there are 12 differences between these two photographs. Can you spot them all?

Circle the differences you find!

Can you spot all

12

differences?

MATCH THE HAZMATS

It's not easy telling these guys apart, but can you match them into pairs? There are five pairs to find.

59

FIND YOUR MOSSINGHAM HOME!

Mossingham is a wonderful place to live, but which property would suit you down to the ground?

Do you like lots of company? — YES / NO

Do you love the outdoors? — NO / YES

Do you mind getting dirty? — NO / YES

NO

Do you like to travel? — YES

NO

Do you like animals? — YES / NO

Could you live in a house with no windows? — NO / YES

YES

YES

Do you love the smell of pizza? — NO

Does your home have to be comfy? — YES / NO

60

MOSSY BOTTOM FARM

You love the great outdoors and don't mind getting your hands dirty. The animals at the farm would be great company, too. Now, let's see if the Farmer has a spare room ...

Do you mind getting up early?

NO

YES

THE FOREST TAKEAWAY

Living above a pizza place wouldn't bother you a bit. You'd help out with deliveries, chat to all the customers and, best of all, take home the leftover pizzas at the end of the night. **YUM!**

Do you like to chat to people?

YES

NO

AGENT RED'S UNDERGROUND
BUNKER

OK, so it's not exactly very cosy, but it's quiet, peaceful, and the neighbours won't bother you because there aren't any!

NO

Are you good at keeping secrets?

YES

FIX MUGG-IN5

Oh dear, it looks like MUGG-IN5 has malfunctioned! Can you work out which pieces are missing and fix him?

D

E

C

F

B

G

A

H

RACE TO THE TOP!

FARMAGEDDON

Shaun has to reach the top of the tower to send a message to Lu-La's home planet. Can you help him to get there? Watch out for Agent Red and other obstacles along the way!

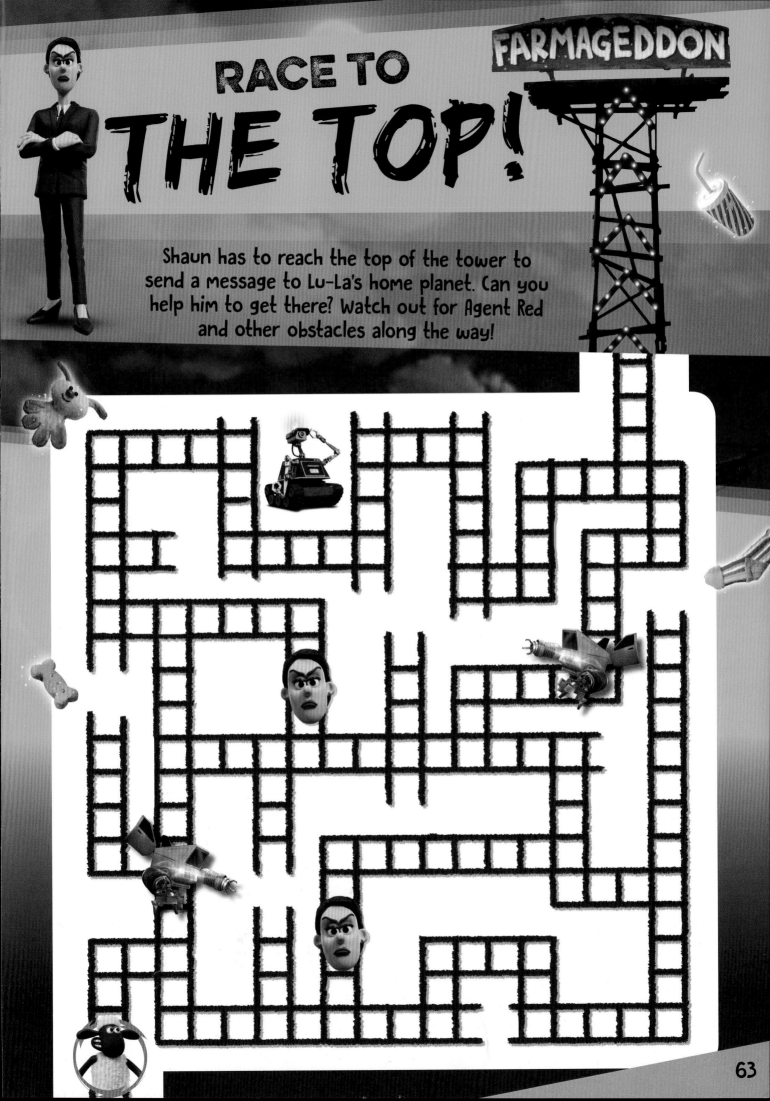

SIGNALS THROUGH SPACE

Lu-La's spaceship was heading for her home, but Shaun overloaded it by ordering too much pizza on its computer system. The spaceship stopped working and hurtled back to Earth.

Lu-La was devastated. How was she going to get home now? Bitzer glared at Shaun and led the alien away. Shaun felt terrible. But then, out of the blue came a faint beeping sound. It was Lu-La's fob! Shaun stared at the flashing symbol on it. It was trying to send a signal to Lu-La's home planet!

The signal bars on the fob needed to reach the top. Shaun glanced at the Farmer's Farmageddon tower. He knew what he had to do, and he needed the Flock's help.

The Flock were ready to pull Shaun up the tower in a basket when Bitzer and Lu-La arrived. Shaun was sure Bitzer would tell him off, but he didn't - he knew Shaun only wanted to help his friend. Lu-La and Shaun made their way up.

BANG! Everyone turned around. What was that? Oh no! Agent Red had tracked the spaceship to Mossy Bottom Farm. She smashed through the theme park, wearing a huge robot suit, and began to climb the tower.

At the top of the swaying tower, Shaun took the fob and held it in the air. **IT WORKED!** The signal went through!

Lu-La and Shaun's joy was short-lived, however. Agent Red was gaining on them. Just as she was about to grab Lu-La, Shaun noticed something flying towards them. **IT WAS BITZER!** He had fired himself from the cannon! As he collided with Agent Red,

SHE LOST HER GRIP ON THE TOWER AND FELL.

Shaun, Lu-La and Bitzer were in trouble too. The tower was falling apart. The three friends looked at each other in terror. They closed their eyes, expecting to fall at any moment ...

But, strangely, they didn't. Something was keeping them in mid-air. A huge beam of light from a spaceship!

The spaceship door opened. Out came two tall aliens. Shaun recognised them from the picture in Lu-La's spaceship. It was her parents, **UB-OO AND ME-MA!** Lu-La ran over and hugged them. Shaun and Bitzer grinned.

It was time for Lu-La to say goodbye. Tears welled in her big purple eyes. Lu-La hugged Shaun and Bitzer and waved goodbye to the Flock. Then, Lu-La, Ub-Oo and Me-Ma boarded the spaceship. Shaun and Bitzer watched as it shot back into the air.

LU-LA WAS FINALLY GOING HOME.

WRITE LU-LA AND SHAUN'S NEXT ADVENTURE

What do you think would happen if Lu-La returned to Earth? Or what if Shaun visited Lu-La on her home planet? Where would they go? Who else would be there?

Could Lu-La and Shaun explore another planet? What would it be called and what strange creatures might live there?

Think of a beginning, middle and end for your story before you begin to write.

Make up your own story here!

_____

_____

_____

_____

_____

_____

_____

_____

_____

_____

Come up
with some
new characters.
They could be
sheep, aliens,
or something
else entirely!

ANSWERS

12. Pick a Pizza Path

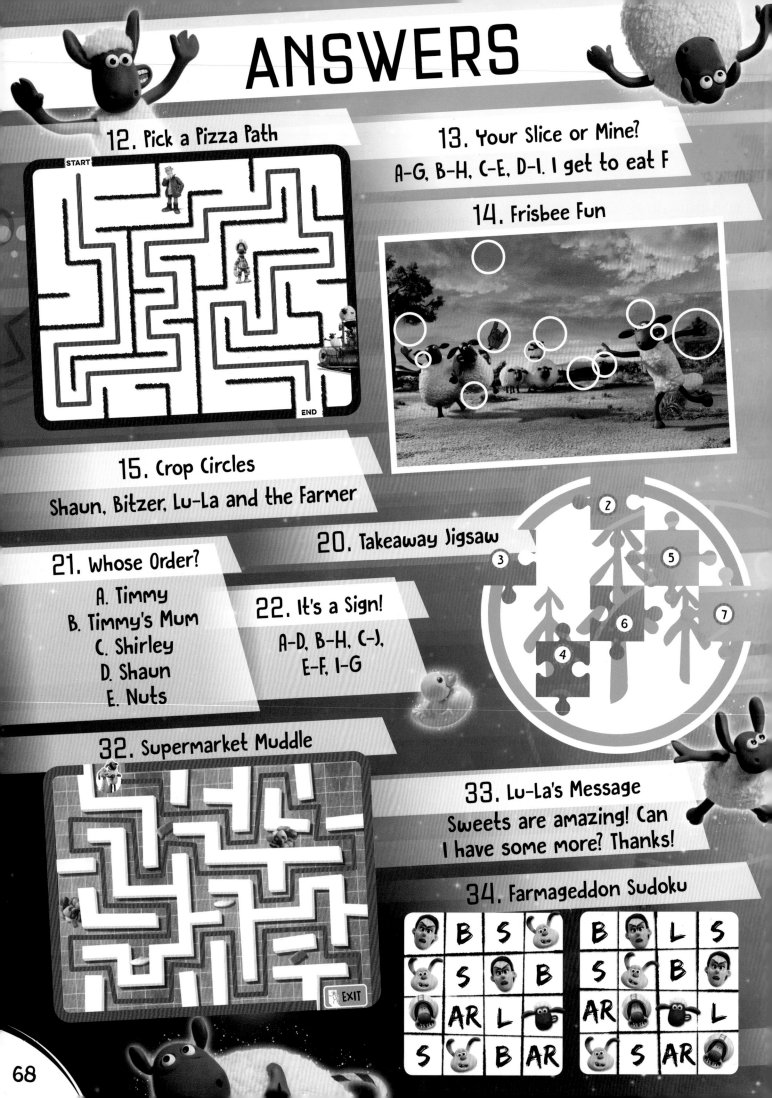

13. Your Slice or Mine?
A-G, B-H, C-E, D-I. I get to eat F

14. Frisbee Fun

15. Crop Circles
Shaun, Bitzer, Lu-La and the Farmer

20. Takeaway Jigsaw

21. Whose Order?
A. Timmy
B. Timmy's Mum
C. Shirley
D. Shaun
E. Nuts

22. It's a Sign!
A-D, B-H, C-J,
E-F, I-G

32. Supermarket Muddle

33. Lu-La's Message
Sweets are amazing! Can
I have some more? Thanks!

34. Farmageddon Sudoku

35. Through the Forest

38. On the Hunt for Differences!

39. Find Lu-La and Shaun

42. Find the Fob!   G

50. Press the Button

51. Error!
Danger! Agent Red and the Hazmats are coming.

52. Top Secret!
Pile One: A, B, D, N, O   Pile Two: G, H, I, L, M
Pile Three: C, E, F, J, K

59. Match the Hazmats
A-G, B-F, C-J, D-I, E-H

58. Selfie Spot

63. Race to the Top!

62. Fix MUGG-IN5
A, B, D, E, G